Rachel's Recital

Written and Illustrated
by
Melinda Green

An Atlantic Monthly Press Book

Little, Brown and Company
Boston   Toronto

FIRST EDITION

Library of Congress Cataloging in Publication Data

Green, Melinda.
  Rachel's recital.

  "An Atlantic Monthly Press book."
  SUMMARY: Rachel, who dislikes piano lessons
so much she won't practice, faces her first
recital unprepared.
  [1. Pianists — Fiction] I. Title.
PZ7.G8252Rac   [Fic]   79-1510
ISBN 0-316-32634-8

ATLANTIC-LITTLE, BROWN BOOKS
ARE PUBLISHED BY
LITTLE, BROWN AND COMPANY
IN ASSOCIATION WITH
THE ATLANTIC MONTHLY PRESS

*Published simultaneously in Canada
by Little, Brown & Company (Canada) Limited*

PRINTED IN THE UNITED STATES OF AMERICA

To Rae Green

Rachel and her brother Benny lived in a red brick apartment house five stories high, which was crowded with people. Families lived above, and families lived below. The people in the apartment house knew everything about everybody else, because the noise came from the floor of one apartment to the ceiling of the other. If Irma would tap-dance, plaster would fall on the tablecloth in Rachel's kitchen.

Two floors down lived a girl named Sonya, who practiced the piano every afternoon. Rachel didn't even notice the music, until one day when her mother said, "That Sonya who lives downstairs plays the piano like a dream."

Rachel ate a cookie and went out to roller-skate.

The next day her mother said, "Just listen to that beautiful piano playing." Then she sighed. "You should only be able to play such beautiful music."

Rachel nodded and took a piece of cake that her mother had just baked. Rachel's mother worked hard in the house, baking and cleaning all day.

"Pick up those crumbs," she said.

Rachel wiped the crumbs with her hand and went outside to play jacks.

The next afternoon, when Rachel came home from school, she heard Sonya's music wafting in through the window. She grabbed a cookie, and was about to run out the door, when her mother said, "Rachel."

Rachel turned around and came to the window where her mother was standing.

"Don't munch your cookie—it will block your ears. Can you hear that beautiful piano playing, Rachel?"

"Yes," said Rachel. "I can hear it."

"Sonya practices every day, so she can play music like a dream. You're going to make music too, Rachel. You're going to be a piano player, and you're going to be famous."

Rachel was not happy to hear those words.

"We don't have a piano," she said, "so how can I play?"

"You'll play," said her mother. "I found a piano teacher three blocks away who has a piano. You can practice at his house."

"I'm very busy already," said Rachel. "I go to school."

"You will go to lessons on Saturday," said her mother. "And every day after school, you will go to your teacher's house to practice. And soon you will be a famous piano player, and you will give concerts."

Rachel went outside and sat down next to Benny, who was shooting marbles on the sidewalk.

"Why is it always me?" she asked.

"What are you talking about?" said Benny.

"Mama's making me take piano lessons," said Rachel. Benny looked at Rachel and started to

laugh. *"You?* Play the piano!" he said. "Ha, ha, ha! Ha, ha, ha, ha, ha!"

Rachel squinted one eye at Benny. "Mama only lets you sit around all day long because you're still a baby." Benny stopped laughing.

"I'm not a baby," he said.

"Yes, you are," said Rachel, and pinched him.

"Well, I got all the talent in the family," said Benny. "You can't even sing on key."

"So what?" said Rachel.

"So . . . *this!*" said Benny. Rachel felt a marble drop down the back of her dress. "I feel sorry for your teacher!" said Benny, and he ran into the apartment before Rachel could hit him.

Rachel and her mother met the piano teacher the next day. His name was Mr. Gratz. Rachel noticed that he had hairy ears, and when he smiled she could see yellow teeth.

In his parlor was a piano, and on the piano was a marble statue of a round face with curly hair like a mane, and beady little eyes, and a mouth that was pinched up at the corners. Was it smiling at her? She looked away. Everywhere there were piles of music books. On the wall there was a shelf holding big leather books: *The Story of Piano, Mozart's Life,* and *A Walk with Music.* The carpet was full of curlicues, and the curtains were thick and green, and had fringes like worms.

Rachel started to back toward the door, but her mother grabbed her hand.

Mr. Gratz sat down on the bench and motioned for Rachel to sit next to him.

Rachel did not move from the doorway. She stood still, rooted to the spot.

Mr. Gratz patted the seat again.

"What's wrong with you?" said her mother. "Are you blind? Mr. Gratz wants you to sit down at the piano."

"I can't," said Rachel.

Mr. Gratz looked confused. He wiped his forehead with a handkerchief.

"What is it?" asked Rachel's mother.

"That face," said Rachel. "It's looking at me."

Mr. Gratz smiled. The bristles stood out on his ears, as he said in a gravelly voice, "That's a bust of Mozart. He's a composer. You don't have to be scared, Rachel. Here—sit down by me."

Rachel went to the bench and sat down. She tried not to look at the bust of Mozart.

"Do just what I do," said Mr. Gratz, and he played three notes on the piano. Rachel heard false teeth clicking when he talked. She turned to look at her mother.

"Go ahead," said her mother.

Rachel swallowed hard and turned back to the piano. She had forgotten which three notes to play. She stared at Mr. Gratz's ears. Then she looked at the bust of Mozart.

"I'll play them again," said Mr. Gratz. His face was red. "Try to pay attention." He played the three notes. Rachel's fingers copied what his fingers did, but a lot slower.

"She's very gifted," said Mr. Gratz. "Here is your book, Rachel. You should practice an hour every day. The first lesson will be tomorrow."

"Do you hear him, Rachel?" said her mother. "An hour every day. After school."

"It's important to practice," said Mr. Gratz.

"Don't even come home after school," said her mother. "Better yet, just run straight to the piano."

When they went home, Rachel said, "I don't want to take piano lessons."

"He is a good teacher," said her mother, "and you will learn from him."

"He has hairy ears," said Rachel, "and that statue of Mozart was smiling at me."

"You're imagining," said her mother. "It's made of marble. It should remind you of how famous you will be if you practice."

17

This was the start of Rachel's new life. Every day she picked up Benny at school. Then she walked home with Edie and Ida. They talked about Ethel's sister, who bleached her hair. They talked about which kids in their class were too short, and why Miriam had a fight with Ruthie. Then Rachel said good-bye to Edie and Ida, and took Benny upstairs to their apartment, dropped her schoolbooks, picked up her piano exercise book, took a cookie, and walked slowly down the stairs.

When she got to the sidewalk she started counting cracks. She counted every crack on each of the three blocks on the way to Mr. Gratz's house. Some days, instead of counting cracks, she looked for birds' nests. She found them in the tops of trees, in the "J" of "JEWEL BAKERY," and over the corners of drainpipes. All around her, children were

CARSON PITT

CHOCOLATIER

553

JEWEL BAKERY

SPECIAL
☆
TODAY
☆
HOT
☆
KNISHES

19

jumping ropes and throwing balls. It seemed like
the whole world was playing, except her.

Then she would reach Mr. Gratz's house. He

was not home on weekday afternoons because he
worked in a music store, selling pianos. Rachel was
supposed to walk inside without knocking.

Before she went into the parlor, she peeked at the bust of Mozart to see if it was smiling at her. When she was sure it wasn't, she ran over to the piano bench and sat down. Peering at the music, she would play a few notes. But then she would notice a little dog running down the street, and

wonder where it was going. That would make her think of her own street, and whether Edie and Ida were playing jacks. "Or they might be roller-skating," she'd think. She'd practice a few more notes, sometimes stepping on the pedals to hear the sounds mash together. "What time is it?" she would wonder, and look around the room for a clock. Before she found a clock, her eyes always met the bust of Mozart. This would remind her of Mr. Gratz's hairy ears, and before she knew it, an hour was up and it was time to go home.

One Saturday Mr. Gratz said, "Rachel, your recital is in two weeks. You will play in a piano quartet—that means there are two pianos on the stage, and three other pupils." His face was red, and he wiped his forehead with his handkerchief. His teeth clicked nervously as he opened the door for her.

"Do me a favor," he said. "Learn the music."

The next afternoon at the piano, it was the same story. As hard as she tried, Rachel could not concentrate on her exercises. She sat down at the piano and thought of a million things. She thought of the boys in her class and which one she liked the best. She thought about interesting ways to draw a dog. She thought about how bored she was. She thought about what kind of cookies her mother was baking. And before she knew it, an hour was up.

At the lesson Mr. Gratz said, "Rachel, have you been practicing?"

"Yes," Rachel answered.

"No, you have not," Mr. Gratz said, and turned red. His teeth clicked. "You have not been practicing, and there is a recital coming up. You will be on stage in front of your mother and father and all of your friends, and if you don't know your music you will be very embarrassed."

"Yes," said Rachel, looking at his ears.

"Did you hear me?" said Mr. Gratz. His voice was more gravelly than ever.

"I practice every day," said Rachel.

"Are you sure?" said Mr. Gratz. "Do you mean you practice the same three notes every day?"

"More than that," said Rachel.

Mr. Gratz cracked his pencil in half. "Then you'll have to practice some more," he said.

Rachel looked at him and folded her hands in her lap. Mr. Gratz glared at her. He took another pencil out of his pocket.

There was a long silence.

"Should I start again?" said Rachel.

"Yes!" shouted Mr. Gratz. His ears were very red. Then he cleared his throat and said quietly, "From the beginning."

When Rachel came home to eat dinner, Sonya was still practicing the piano. Irma was tap-dancing overhead.

"Beautiful," said Rachel's mother, passing a dish of peas and lamb chops across the table. "I hope you are coming along as beautifully. I spoke to your teacher just the other week."

Rachel dropped some peas in her lap. Benny looked at her. Rachel's father kept eating.

"He says you are doing very well."

Rachel swallowed.

"Of course, for the price of those lessons, I would tell a mother the same thing."

Rachel looked into her lap. She tried to put the peas back into her spoon.

"For the recital, I'm very excited," said Rachel's mother. "I invited everybody." She passed Rachel the vegetables. "You don't look so good," she said. "Better eat some turnip greens."

Rachel was getting very nervous. Her aunt made her a new dress just for the recital. It had ruffles and a pink bow in back. Rachel didn't dare tell anybody that she didn't know how to play her piece. Her mother often asked Mr. Gratz how Rachel was doing, and every time he answered, "Fine! Fine!"

The day before the recital, Rachel came home from school and went into her bedroom. "What am I going to do?" she thought. "It's too late to learn to play my piece, and Mama will really yell when she finds out I don't know how." She started to cry, dripping tears on the middle of the bedroom floor. Then suddenly she had an idea. She wiped her eyes on her dress and opened the bedroom door.

"Oh, Benny!" she said sweetly.

Benny was in the kitchen. "What do you want?" he said.

"Let's go to the candy store," said Rachel, "and I'll buy you some jawbreakers."

"Really?" said Benny, coming out of the kitchen.

"Yes!" said Rachel. "And all you have to do is put a jawbreaker in each cheek and pretend you have the mumps."

"Why?" said Benny. "Why can't I eat them?"

"You can eat them afterward," said Rachel.

"Are you sure Mama won't get mad?" said Benny.

"It's just a joke," said Rachel. "She'll think it's funny."

"Oh. All right," said Benny.

Rachel bought two big jawbreakers and put them in Benny's mouth. "I can't talk," mumbled Benny.

"That's okay," said Rachel. She took Benny's hand, and led him into the dining room, where her mother was sitting. "Look, Mama! Benny's cheeks are all puffed up! He must be sick!"

"Looks like the mumps," said her mother. She put her hand on Benny's forehead. "Are you hot?"

"Mumph," said Benny.

"He can hardly talk!" said their mother.

"If he has the mumps, then I probably caught them, too," said Rachel. "And I could infect all the people at the recital. It wouldn't be fair." Rachel went into her bedroom and lay down on the bed.

Their mother snapped Benny's suspenders and

took her coat and hat off the hook. "We're going
to the doctor right this minute," she said. Then she
turned around to close the window.

At that moment, a jawbreaker fell out of Benny's
mouth and rolled across the floor. Rachel sat up
in bed.

"What was that?" said his mother. She saw that one of Benny's cheeks was flat. A big blue jaw-breaker rolled past the table. "Benny! Playing a joke!" said their mother. She grabbed him by the back of his neck. "Playing a joke like this the day before Rachel's concert!" She smacked him on his behind. The other jawbreaker shot out of his mouth and bounced across the table. "I've seen rotten things, but to pretend you're sick! At such an important time! You go in there right now and apologize to Rachel!"

Benny walked into the bedroom. "So, it wasn't such a good idea," said Rachel.

At her lesson Rachel played the beginning of the piece, and then stopped as soon as she got to the next line, which she had never practiced.

"Why do you stop?" shouted Mr. Gratz, his strands of gray hair bouncing on his forehead.

"This is the part I don't know so well," said Rachel.

"The recital is tomorrow," he wheezed. "And you must not only learn how to play this piece—you must *memorize* it!" The bristles stood out on his ears. "I have never had a pupil like you in my life, and I have been teaching for twenty-five years!" He put his face in his hands.

Rachel looked at the bust of Mozart, and felt a twinge in her stomach. Then she looked at Mr. Gratz. "I wonder if he had hairy ears when he was my age," she thought.

On the day of the recital Rachel woke up shaking. Her heart was beating twice as fast as usual, and her hands felt like ice. All morning her stomach was turning. But there was no getting out of it.

"Should I tell Mama now?" she thought, as she put on her pink dress. "Should I go to the auditorium and then disappear?"

The whole family walked to the recital in their best clothes. Rachel thought and thought. Every solution seemed worse than the one before. "I'm going to get a spanking till I'm black and blue," thought Rachel.

"You look like a princess," said her mother. "I know you will make me very proud tonight. Week after week you have been practicing, and now you will show us what this has all been for." Her mother fixed the bow on Rachel's dress. "Pull up your socks," she said.

"Good luck, Rachel," said her father, and gave her a kiss.

"It's time to go on stage!" said Mr. Gratz.

Rachel thought she would faint. She couldn't move. "What am I going to do? What am I going to do?" she thought.

From out of the crowd of friends and parents in the auditorium came the three other pupils who were to perform. Everyone else sat down in the audience. Mr. Gratz looked at Rachel. His teeth clicked. "Play well," he said to each of them. To Rachel he growled, "Good luck."

Rachel felt the stage lights on her face. She couldn't see the audience, but she heard them rattling their programs. "I won't be scared," she thought. "I'll just do the best I can." Two of the pupils were smiling, and the other one was biting his nails. Rachel was shaking. The black pianos gleamed, and the wooden planks of the stage floor shone under her feet. The pupils sat down at their assigned places at the pianos. Mr. Gratz stood in the center. He raised his hand in the air and counted, one ... two ... three ...

Then they began to play. Rachel played the first two lines, which had stuck in her mind from practicing. But after that her mind was a blank. Suddenly she realized that the music was going on

without her. So she smiled at the audience. She threw her hands here and there. Her fingers moved all over the piano without pressing the keys. She tapped her feet and bobbed her head. The girl next to her looked at her strangely a few times, but Rachel paid no attention.

"If I keep moving," she thought, "maybe nobody will know the difference." The music went on and on. "Oh, no. It's starting to repeat," she thought. She smiled again at the audience. Her hands moved up the keyboard and down.

Finally the piece was over. There was thunderous applause. Rachel stood up and bowed. Her knees were knocking together. She could hardly walk backstage with the other pupils.

The violin students went on next. Rachel sat behind the curtain, watching. Her heart was pounding so hard that she could barely hear.

The girl who had played the piano beside Rachel was looking at her. At last she said, "Were you playing the piano, or not?"

Rachel looked offended. "Of course," she said.
"Excuse me," said the girl, and turned red.

After the recital was over, Rachel's mother and
father and friends ran over to congratulate her.
"You were very good," said her father.

"You have a great presence," said her mother. "You were born for the stage."

Mr. Gratz stayed on the other side of the room. It was so crowded with people that Rachel's mother didn't have a chance to say a word to him.

After all the relatives and neighbors had congratulated Rachel, the family went out for ice cream. Benny ate a whole banana split by himself, but Rachel hardly looked at her sundae. She felt that she didn't deserve it. The whole family was eating ice cream for nothing. She felt bad because Mr. Gratz was so angry at her. She felt bad because her mother was so proud of her. She felt especially bad because she had not slept all week. But she was very happy the recital was over.

"Rachel," said her mother, "that was very beautiful music." Rachel nodded her head. "But I don't think you'll be taking lessons anymore."

Rachel's eyes opened wide.

"Papa and I decided that with your energy and stage presence you could be a good dancer. You will take dancing lessons, and you will practice, and someday you will be famous."

Rachel nodded her head and started to eat her ice cream.

"Benny, you will take the violin."

Benny choked on a slice of banana.

On the way home, Rachel looked at the stars and hardly said anything. All the relatives talked and talked.

"Rachel did a wonderful job," said her aunt. "I'm sure her teacher will be sorry to see her go."

"He has other pupils," said Rachel.

"I can't wait to talk to him about the recital," said Rachel's mother.

Rachel's stomach dropped. Her voice came out in a squeak. "I can't wait to start dancing lessons!" she said.

"And Benny has a talent like Rachel," said their mother. "He will be a fine musician."

Rachel pinched Benny. He stepped on her toe.

"Such wonderful children!" said Rachel's aunt.